TATTOO TALES™
SKIN CRAWLERS

By Cathy Dubowski
Illustrated by Jean Cassels

Random House 🏠 New York

CONTENTS

INTRODUCTION

Bugs are everywhere—in houses and yards, in forests and fields. They can be found in the hottest jungles of Africa and in the snow and ice of the Antarctic.

Bugs outnumber people—by far. In fact, there are more bugs in the world than any other living creature we can see. Scientists have identified more than a million different kinds. But they think this may only be a tiny percentage of what's really out there creeping and crawling around the world.

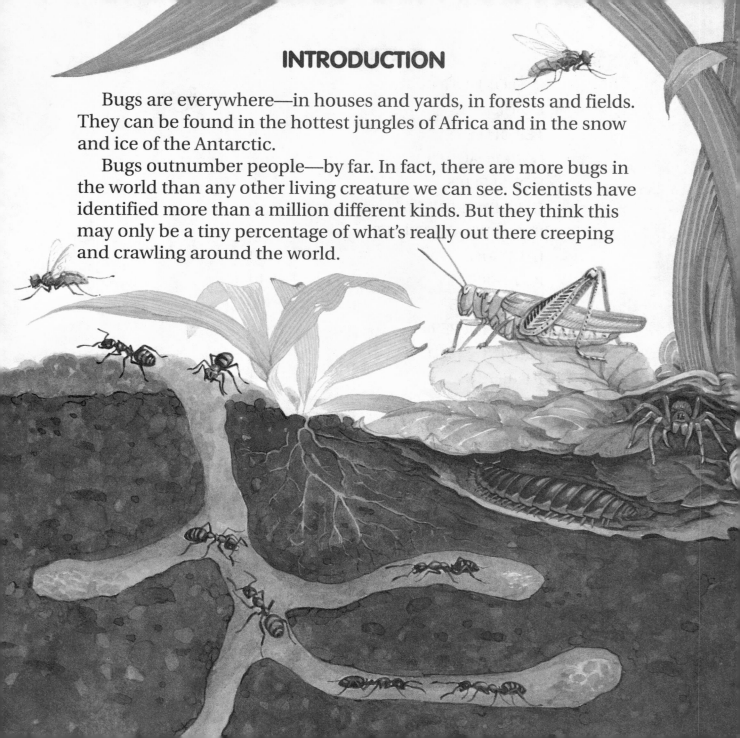

Do bugs make your skin crawl? Sure they do. But many bugs
are a big help to people and the environment, too.
Besides, humans are the new kids on the block.
Bugs have been on earth for more
than 400 million years.

BLACK ANTS

Most bugs like to live outside. But there are some that like living in your house even better! Little black ants come inside looking for sweet things to eat. When they find food, they go back to their nests, leaving an invisible trail that other ants can smell. Then all their family and friends can follow the scent trail and join the feast!

TERMITES

Termites like to eat wood. If no one stops them, a colony of these tiny creatures can destroy an entire house.

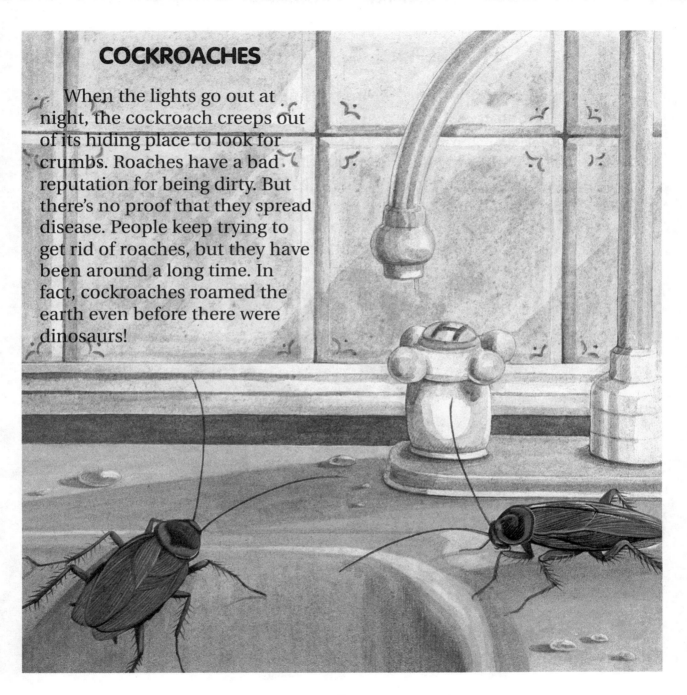

COCKROACHES

When the lights go out at night, the cockroach creeps out of its hiding place to look for crumbs. Roaches have a bad reputation for being dirty. But there's no proof that they spread disease. People keep trying to get rid of roaches, but they have been around a long time. In fact, cockroaches roamed the earth even before there were dinosaurs!

HOUSEFLIES

Houseflies eat anything—from rotting garbage to manure—then leave some of their "spit" behind. Maybe even on your dinner! That's one way flies spread filth and disease. Bluebottle and greenbottle flies lay their eggs in dead and decaying matter. The hatched maggots feed on the material. That helps break it down and recycle it back into the earth.

GARDEN SPIDERS

Fear of spiders is called *arachnophobia*. But don't worry: Most of the spiders you find in your house and yard are harmless. Garden spiders spin silken webs to catch insects such as flies. But they don't chew them up. They inject them with a fluid that liquefies them. Then the spiders slurp up the fluid as if it were soup.

BLACK WIDOW SPIDERS

Female black widow spiders *are* poisonous. You can tell the males and females apart by their markings. Females have a yellow or red hourglass shape on their abdomen, while the males have white or red markings on their sides. The name comes from their dating habits. After mating, the female eats the male!

LADYBUGS

Some of the prettiest bugs are excellent "gardeners." Ladybugs, or ladybird beetles, help gardeners and farmers by eating insects that destroy plants and crops.

BUTTERFLIES

Butterflies carry pollen from flower to flower. In the fall, hundreds of thousands of monarch butterflies migrate thousands of miles to southern California or Mexico.

HONEYBEES

Honeybees pollinate flowers as they gather nectar. They turn the nectar into honey and store it in honeycombs made of beeswax. People have kept bees for centuries in order to harvest their honey. The beeswax is used for candles and in polishes and cosmetics. In some parts of the world, people eat toasted honeybees!

GRASSHOPPER

You may not see a grasshopper till—*boing!*—it jumps in the air. It can jump up to 20 times its body length. That's like you jumping to the top of a seven-story building!

PRAYING MANTIS

The praying mantis looks so innocent, as if it is saying its prayers—but watch out! It's just waiting patiently in the green grass and leaves to ambush its next meal! Praying mantises in the garden will eat many bugs that would have destroyed your plants. But they sometimes turn into cannibals and eat each other!

JUNE BUG

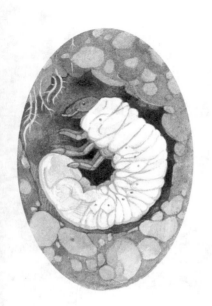

The June bug begins life in the fall as a worm, or grub, that burrows underground. It remains there for several years, turning into a beetle. Then, around June, it comes to the surface. Now its back is covered with hard plates that protect like armor. This hard wing cover makes a loud buzz as it flies from tree to tree.

STINK BUG

The stink bug leaves a bad smell wherever it goes—especially when it gets squashed. But there are some birds that eat stink bugs anyway!

MILLIPEDE

The millipede's name means "thousand feet." But it can't really run very fast from danger. Instead, it protects itself by curling up into a hard little ball.

MOSQUITO

The female mosquito zooms in to stick a long needlelike tube into a person's skin. Then she injects a fluid that thins the blood so she can suck it up. Most people are allergic to this fluid, which is why they get those itchy bumps. The mosquito doesn't drink the blood, though. She uses it to feed the eggs inside her.

DRAGONFLIES

The fastest airborne bug is the dragonfly. Some can fly up to 60 miles per hour! The dragonfly can also hover in the air, fly backward, and stop on a dime.

The dragonfly has two sets of wings. But unlike the butterfly's wings, these don't flap together. When one pair goes up, the other pair goes down. Dragonflies are good to have around because they eat mosquitoes. In fact, the dragonfly's nickname is the "mosquito hawk."

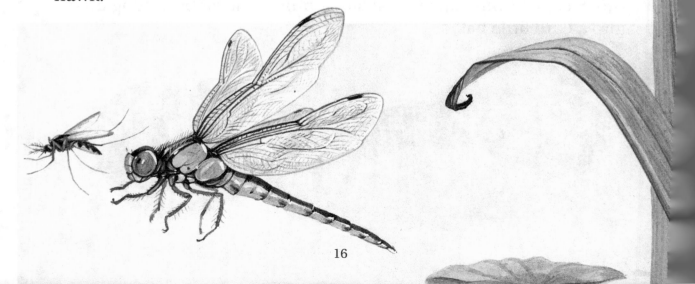

16

BANDED WOOLLY-BEAR

The banded woolly-bear is the caterpillar stage of an Isabella tiger moth. Legend has it that woolly-bears can predict how harsh the winter will be. The thicker the hair, the colder the winter!

CRICKET

Want to know the temperature? Some people say that a cricket can tell you. Just count how many times a cricket chirps in 14 seconds. Add 40. That's the temperature in degrees Fahrenheit.

TARANTULA

The big hairy tarantula looks as if it belongs in a haunted house! It gets its name from a wild Italian dance, the tarantella, that was supposed to be a "cure" for a spider bite. Though the tarantula looks scary, it's not poisonous and eats only other insects and small animals.

KILLER BEES

African honeybees have bad tempers! They were imported to Brazil from Africa to improve the honey-making industry. People named them *abelhas assassinas*—which is Portuguese for "killer bees"! The bees thrived and have been spreading north ever since. And so has their scary reputation! Killer bees have an ordinary sting—they're just more likely to use it, and they attack in large swarms. They have killed people and animals that have disturbed their hives.

FIREFLIES

Fireflies bring magic to a summer night. Like twinkling stars, fireflies—or lightning bugs—blink through the darkness to signal each other. That greenish yellow light has stumped scientists for years. Most light creates heat. But the glow of a firefly is a "cold" light. No one knows why. But the firefly's secret could help us develop ways to save energy.

LUNA MOTH

Luna means "moon"—and it's the light of the moon that the luna moth and most other moths navigate by. They are often fooled by electric lights—that's why you see them hovering around your back-porch light at night!

MAN-FACED BUG

This bug gives birds a fright in Southeast Asia! It has bright colors and strange markings that make it look a lot like the face of a person.